Mr. Turtle meets Ms. Ladybug

Written and Illustrated by George Blevins

PUBLISHED BY CAROUSEL OF HAPPINESS BOOKS

First edition
ISBN 978-0-9891551-0-6

Additional copies of this book
are available from:
Carousel of Happiness Books
P. O. Box 431
Nederland CO 80426
carouselofhappinessbooks@gmail.com

Printed by Publication Printers Corp.
2001 S. Platte River Dr.
Denver CO 80223

Mr. Turtle always looked grumpy when he had to go outside.

He was looking grumpy the day he almost stepped on Ms. Ladybug.

"You are about to step on me," she pointed out.

Mr. Turtle stopped in mid-stride and considered this remark.

He looked down.

"Would you like some tea?" asked she. "I've eaten all the toast."

"I would prefer tea at home," he answered.

"How far from home are you? Is it close by?"

Mr. Turtle made an awful snorting noise, which she later learned was his laugh.

He drew his long neck back into his shell, until finally even his head had disappeared.

"This is home," came his voice. "Won't you come in?"

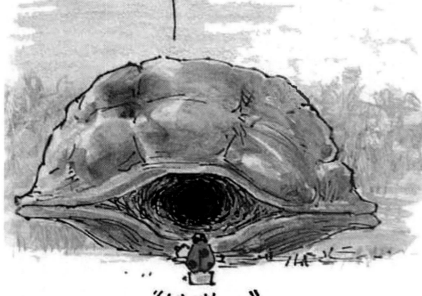

"Well..."

"Nothing ventured, nothing gained," she told herself.

"A journey of a thousand miles begins with a single step," she said.

"If you never try, you never know."

And she climbed into the opening.

She could see
absolutely nothing,
but up ahead she
could hear the rattle
of tea things.

She followed
the sounds.

She stepped into a softly-lit kitchen.
Mr. Turtle was putting a pot of tea
in the center of the kitchen table.
"Please sit down," he said. "I hope
you like Darjeeling."

"Why, you are
almost as small as
I am!" said she.

"Indoors it's safe to be small." he explained. "If I had my way, I'd never set foot outside."

"There are risks, to be sure," she replied, "but there are things to appreciate, too. The tea smells delicious."

"There are these little cookies to go with it," he said, sliding the plate toward her.

They talked and talked, never noticing the time, until Ms. Ladybug suddenly said,

"My goodness! It's getting toward mid-day!"

"So it is," he said. "Let's have a little lunch, shall we?"

"Much as I'd love to, I have a thousand things to do," she said. "Another time?"

"Tomorrow if you like."

"Tomorrow it is then," she said, and away she flew, off to do the thousand things or at least some part of them.

Mr. Turtle watched her go, fairly confident that they would meet again soon. And so they did, the next morning and many mornings after.

They quickly fell into a morning routine that could be counted on to remain comfortably unchanging.

A few things did change, of course. Sometimes he wore his orange bathrobe instead of the blue.

And sometimes they had Earl Grey instead of Darjeeling.

But the principle difference was in their conversation. Though they talked slowly (especially Mr. Turtle), with frequent long pauses, in time they talked about everything they could imagine.

She talked about interesting things she had seen -

dragonflies suddenly stopping in midair,

the swirling centers of sunflowers,

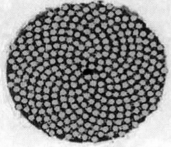

the sun making its settings and risings so pretty by shining on the undersides of clouds,

and the bright star that shows first each evening and last each morning.

"That's Venus," he told her. "It isn't a star at all. It's a planet. I read it in a book." And he showed her his library.

"Who would have thought a turtle would have a library inside his shell," she marveled. He pulled out a book.

"Here are pictures of stars. Billions of them, all too far away for either of us to see.

And here are pictures of creatures too tiny for our own eyes ever to see."
She marveled again.

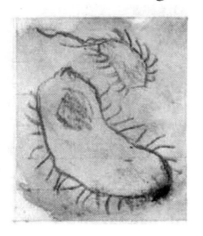

He bent closer. "Besides," he whispered, "I really am afraid to go outside."

"I'd really rather stay home and get my news of the outside world from you."

She raised her cup. "Happy to do what I can. Just keep in mind that my sort lasts only a matter of months and I'm eight weeks old already."

"Your sort?" —

— "Bugs! Turtles live for years, bugs about a season."

"Oh," he said. He did not know what else to say. He had never thought of this.

He offered her another cupcake.

"I really shouldn't," she said, and did.

Sometimes, though not often, they went for a walk. "I can't decide whether I feel safer in the daytime," he said, "when I can see the dangers, or at night, when they can't see me."

Ms. Ladybug made it a habit to distract him from his fears when she could.

"See how much brighter the sky looks between the trees? Do you suppose it really is?"

The next morning at teatime they looked it up. As it turned out, the sky simply looked brighter because the dark trees framed it.

"Something new every day," she said.

"New and wonderful," said he.

So their summer went. Each day was delightful and followed by another.

(This page is for you to color)

They discovered the wonders of the microscope.

They read each other silly stories.

They made mobiles,

learned to Samba,

and had more adventures and epiphanies (look it up, they would have) than there is space to tell.

15

"I have never known a nicer summer," she said one day.

"Ha! Can't fool me on that one. This is your first," he said.

"True enough," she said with a sigh. "And how the days have flown. Each as quickly and as pleasantly as this one. Look at the time! I really must fly myself!"

"Still haven't got the thousand things done yet?"

"Only a few things left," she said. And with that she took to the air.

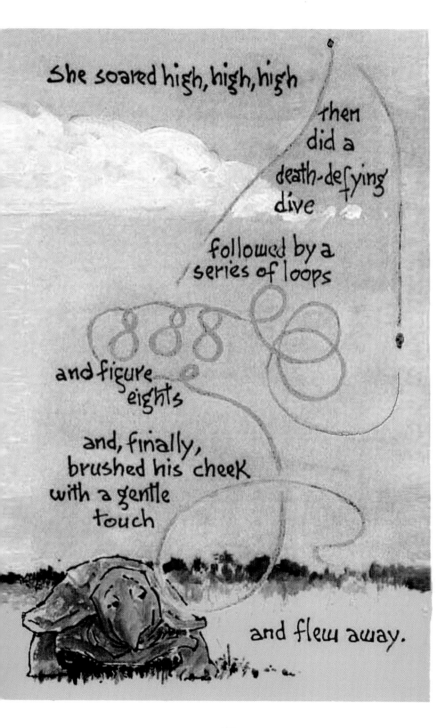

She soared high, high, high

then did a death-defying dive

followed by a series of loops

and figure eights

and, finally, brushed his cheek with a gentle touch

and flew away.

The next morning she did not appear,

nor the next

 nor the next, nor the one after that,

until slowly Mr. Turtle began to accept that Ms. Ladybug's short season had ended.

For a long time - many,
many endless days - he was
sadder than words can say.
He sat in his shell, went out
only when he had to, and spent
much time recalling the things
they had done together.

Then one evening, wandering
aimlessly, he happened to glance
toward his front entry and saw

the moon rising over the trees.
"If you were here," he heard
himself say, "we would go
have a better look at that."

And that is exactly what he did.

Mr. Turtle lived on for many years, as turtles do, and bravely explored many things in the great world, though he never thought himself particularly brave.

As he once in his later years said to Ms. Ladybug, "I've certainly learned a lot since you left, but nicest of all was learning that good friends never really go away.

Part of them moves in."

For Chloe Anna Switzer, with love.